Jeremy Strong

The Indoor Pirates on
Treasure Island

Illustrated by Nick Sharratt

PUFFIN BOOKS

This is for Jack

PUFFIN BOOKS

Published by the Penguin Group
Penguin Books Ltd, 27 Wrights Lane, London W8 5TZ, England
Penguin Putnam Inc., 375 Hudson Street, New York, New York 10014, USA
Penguin Books Australia Ltd, Ringwood, Victoria, Australia
Penguin Books Canada Ltd, 10 Alcorn Avenue, Toronto, Ontario, Canada M4V 3B2
Penguin Books (NZ) Ltd, 182–190 Wairau Road, Auckland 10, New Zealand

Penguin Books Ltd, Registered Offices: Harmondsworth, Middlesex, England

First published 1998
9 10 8

Typeset in Monotype Baskerville

Made and printed in England by Clays Ltd, St Ives plc

British Library Cataloguing in Publication Data
A CIP catalogue record for this book is available from the British Library

ISBN 0–140–38637–8

Contents

1 An Introduction to the Indoor Pirates

There were lots of things the Indoor Pirates didn't like. They didn't like the sea, because it was wet. They didn't like the rain, because that was wet too. And they didn't like bathing much, because that was very, VERY wet.

They didn't even like going on boats because they got collywobbles in their stomachs. (But they did like playing with boats in the bath.) It was because they didn't like the sea or boats that they lived in a house, and that was why they were called the Indoor Pirates – because they lived indoors, of course, at number 25 Dolphin Street.

There were five pirates altogether, with Captain Blackpatch as the leader. He had a thin pointy beard, a thin pointy moustache, and a thin pointy nose. He had a proper black patch too, even though it was on the torn sleeve of his jacket and not over one eye like most pirate captains. Captain Blackpatch reckoned he was a very good captain, and he gave

orders to his crew in a gruff, captain-ing kind of voice. Then he'd sneak off and have a little nap while everyone else worked.

There were two girl pirates, and their names were Molly and Polly. They were twins and they spent most of their time arguing with each other. They could argue about absolutely anything, and they would too. Molly might say, 'I can run faster than you.'

And Polly would say, 'So? SO?! I can run slower than you!'

That was just the sort of silly quarrel they liked to have. On and on they'd go, arguing about their hair, or how prongy their forks were, or how much fizz they had in their drink – until Captain Blackpatch got so cross he'd make them walk the plank. Even then Polly and Molly carried on arguing.

'You go first.'

'No – *you* go first.'

'I'll go first if you go in front of me!'

Eventually Blackpatch would get so fed up with listening to them, he would put on his earphones and turn up his Walkman. (Captain Blackpatch liked listening to *101 Sea Songs for Landlubbers*.)

Bald Ben was First Mate. He had huge muscles and was so strong he could lift up an armchair with one arm. (I don't mean the armchair had one arm – I mean Bald Ben only needed one arm to lift it up.) Bald Ben wasn't totally bald. He did have *something* on his head, and that was a tattoo of a red rose. Underneath the rose was a message: I LOVE MUM.

The fifth Indoor Pirate was Lumpy Lawson. He was tall and thin and he was Chief Cook and Scrubber-Upper. Sadly, he was not terribly good at cooking. Lumpy Lawson's gravy had more lumps in it than a bag of potatoes. When he got upset about something he also had a habit of shouting out very bad words, like 'jigglepoops!'

Although they didn't like boats or the sea, the pirates had made the inside of their house just like a boat. There were no stairs, just rope rigging to climb up and down. They had painted the walls blue with fluffy white clouds. There were several plastic seagulls hanging from the ceilings.

The pirates thought that living in a house was much better than being on a boat. For one thing, they could go to the shops and the park whenever they wanted. The Indoor

Pirates liked going to the park because there was a big climbing frame there built in the shape of a pirate ship. They didn't get seasick when they went on this pirate ship, and if it rained they could run home before they got too wet.

Of course, the Indoor Pirates tried to pretend they weren't pirates at all. It was supposed to be a secret, but everyone knew because there was a big black Jolly Roger flying from the chimney pot of number 25 and, in any case, they dressed like pirates. The milkman knew straight away.

'You're a pirate, aren't you?' he asked Captain Blackpatch.

'No, I'm not!'

'Yes you are. You're wearing a pirate

captain's hat and pirate clothes. You must
be a pirate.'

'No I'm not!' growled Captain
Blackpatch.

'What are you then?'

'I'm . . . I'm . . . I'm a bank manager!'
declared Blackpatch.

'A bank manager! Don't be silly. Bank
managers don't wear pirate costumes.'

'We're having a fancy dress party at the
bank,' the Captain claimed rather lamely.

'Oh yes?' The milkman raised his
eyebrows. 'And my name's Snow White.'

Captain Blackpatch gazed back haughtily.
'I think that's a very silly name for a
milkman,' he said,
snatching two
pints of milk from
the milkman and
slamming the
door.

Despite all the pretence, the neighbours quite liked the pirates. Mrs Bishop, who lived at number 27, was especially fond of Bald Ben. He often carried her shopping bags home for her. Sometimes she cut flowers from her garden and gave them to him, and sometimes she made all the pirates little cakes and biscuits. The pirates loved Mrs Bishop's cakes and biscuits because they didn't have lumps in them, unlike the ones Lumpy Lawson made.

Life at number 25 Dolphin Street had been going along fairly smoothly for some time, until the day Captain Blackpatch went into town because he had run out of jelly babies. He bought some more without any trouble, but he missed the bus back from the shops, and had to wait over an hour, *in the rain*, and came back soaked to the skin.

He stood in the hall with water dripping from his hat, his nose, his hair, his beard, his arms and all his clothes. A large pool of water collected around his feet. 'The bus never came!' he  roared. 'I could have got home more quickly if I'd walked!'

'Why didn't you?' asked Lumpy Lawson, and a very sensible question it was too.

Blackpatch ignored him. He pulled off his coat and wrung it out. 'I shall tell you one thing – I am never going to wait for a bus again, and I am never going to stand in the rain like that again either.'

'That's two things,' said Bald Ben. 'You

said you'd only tell us one thing. Which of those two things do you want us to listen to?'

Captain Blackpatch shot a murderous glance at him, but Bald Ben was much stronger than he was so he decided not to murder him after all. 'And,' the Captain went on, 'I am going to learn to drive.'

'That's three things . . .' Bald Ben began.

'Stop arguing with me! You're even worse than Molly and Polly!'

'No he's not,' said Polly.

'No he is,' said Molly. 'He's the worstest . . . er . . . the worsting worserer . . . I mean the worsingest . . . Oh bother, I give up!'

Captain Blackpatch jumped on to the table, drew his wooden sword and waved it at them threateningly. 'Wobbling walruses! Will you listen? I am going to learn to drive a car. Then we shan't need to wait for buses any longer and we can go just where we like. Tomorrow morning, when I am nice and dry, we shall go to the garage and buy a car.'

And that is exactly what they did. The garage man was a little scared when he found himself surrounded by pirates, but he was glad to get rid of one of his rather battered vehicles. Captain Blackpatch fixed his eyes on a small truck. It was blood red, which was an excellent pirate colour, and it had a cabin at the front big enough for two people, and an open space at the back for carrying loads, a bit like the deck of a boat.

'That will do nicely,' said the Captain,

turning to the garage man. 'How many cannons does it have?'

'Cannons?' The garage man shook his head. 'What do you want cannons for?'

'For battles, of course.'

'I think you'll find that other trucks don't have cannons, so I'm sure you'll be all right.'

'Hmmmm. Well, I shall only buy it if you paint a skull and crossbones on each door, *and* I want a Jolly Roger flying from the aerial. It needs an anchor as well.'

'An anchor?'

'Yes, an anchor so that I can make it stop.'

'But it's got new brakes,' explained the garage man.

'I don't think you heard me,' growled the Captain. 'I won't buy it without the skull and crossbones, a pirate flag, *and* an anchor.'

The garage man sighed and said he'd find an anchor. He also arranged to deliver the truck to the house since Blackpatch couldn't actually drive yet. In the meantime, the Indoor Pirates went home so that the Captain could arrange his first driving lesson.

'When we go out in the truck,' said Polly, 'I'm going to sit in the front.'

'You'll have to sit on *me* then,' snarled Molly, 'because I'm getting in the front before you.'

The Captain drew his sword and said that nobody was going to sit up front, except him. 'You lot can all sit in the back,' he declared.

'But we might get wet,' Bald Ben pointed out.

'Good. Maybe it will make your hair grow,' snapped Blackpatch, and then picked up the telephone so that he could arrange some driving lessons. Although he sounded rather grumpy, he was secretly looking forward to driving his pirate truck.

2 A Testing Time

The next day Mr Crock the driving
instructor knocked at number 25. When
Blackpatch opened the front door, Mr
Crock took one look and jumped back a
step. 'Goodness me, you're a pirate!'

'No I'm not,' scowled Blackpatch. 'I'm a
bank manager.'

The instructor burst out laughing. 'If
you're a bank manager my
name's Snow White!'

'Don't be stupid,'
grunted the Captain.
'The milkman's Snow
White. Now, teach me
how to drive.'

The Indoor Pirates
went rushing outside and
leaned over the garden

wall cheering while Mr Crock and the Captain climbed into the truck. The engine rattled and roared. The exhaust pipe sent out a puff of blue smoke and burped very loudly.

'It *has* got a cannon!' cried Captain Blackpatch with delight, as the other pirates dived for cover and fell higgledy-piggledy on top of each other. 'I heard it go bang!'

'I think it backfired,' murmured Mr Crock.

'Don't be daft. Cannons can't backfire. You might be a driving instructor but I don't think you're very bright. Do you know

what would happen if cannons *did* backfire? We'd end up shooting ourselves. What's the point in doing that?'

Mr Crock didn't have an answer to this, so he meekly suggested that they got going.

'Full speed ahead!' cried Captain Blackpatch and off they went,

with a *jolt*,

and a *judder*,

and a *jerk*,

and a *jump*.

The driving instructor clung to his seat as Captain Blackpatch went sailing down the road at an ever-increasing speed. The first corner was coming up fast.

'I think now would be a good time to try an emergency stop,' shouted Mr Crock.

'OK – anchors away!' shouted the Captain and he hurled the anchor out through the window so that it hooked round a passing lamp-post.

Unfortunately, the anchor was attached to the rear bumper, and as soon as the chain was paid out there was a sickening KERRUNCH! and the bumper was torn off the back. The truck went careering on and there was a second sickening KERRUNCH! – as it finally managed to stop by ploughing straight into a rather stout and sturdy tree.

After that first little drive, Captain Blackpatch had to wait a week for his next lesson because the truck was in the garage, recovering from its bruises, and Mr Crock was in bed at home, recovering from *his* bruises.

When Blackpatch did have another lesson, Mr Crock started by carefully showing his pirate-pupil the brake and explaining what it was, what it did, and how to use it. From then on, the Captain's driving improved rapidly and soon Mr Crock decided that Captain Blackpatch was ready to take his driving test.

'You'd better get your friends to help you learn the Highway Code,' he suggested.

The Indoor Pirates enjoyed testing the Captain. Their glorious leader sat on a chair in the middle of the room, surrounded by the crew who fired questions at him very fiercely, as if he was their prisoner and they were trying to find out where the hidden treasure was.

'What should you always do before you start driving?' asked Molly.

'Switch the engine on.'

'No, something else.'

'Shut the door.'

'No, something else,' insisted Molly.

'Er, take off the handbrake?'

'No, something else . . .'

'Blow your nose?'

'No, something –'

'I DON'T KNOW!' exploded Captain Blackpatch. 'Tell me, you idiot!'

'Look in your mirror, signal, then pull out.'

'Why should I look in my mirror? To see if my lipstick's on properly? I'm not a girly!'

Polly pointed at her twin sister. 'You're a girly!'

'Yeah – and you're a boyly!' sneered Molly.

'A boyly! What's a boyly meant to be?' Polly demanded.

'It's what you are,' snapped Molly, who hadn't got a clue what she was talking about – and neither had anyone else.

'What does a triangular sign mean with a picture of a cow?' asked Bald Ben.

'Low-flying cows.'

'Wrong!' shouted Bald Ben happily. 'Now you have to start again.' Ben made it sound as if they were playing snakes and ladders.

Captain Blackpatch got to his feet. 'I'm not putting up with any more of this,' he sulked. 'I'm going to bed. Nobody around here seems to appreciate who's been putting in all the work. I have been learning to drive, and with good reason because I have got a plan. In fact, it's more of a treat than a plan. If I fail my test tomorrow then you'll all be sorry. So there.'

And Blackpatch clambered up the rope rigging to his bedroom, leaving the other pirates wondering what sort of treat their captain had in mind.

Captain Blackpatch was very surprised when he met the driving-test examiner. 'You're a woman!' he cried.

Mrs Broadside ticked a little box on her examination sheet. 'Well done,' she murmured. 'You have just passed the eyesight test. Shall we go? What should you do first, before you start?'

'Er, check my lipstick.'

'I beg your pardon?'

'I mean, mirror, signal and move off.'

'Good. Off we go then. What an interesting vehicle. I like the skull and crossbones.' Mrs Broadside glanced at the Captain. 'You must be a pirate.'

'No, I'm a bank manager.'

'Really? I suppose it's much the same thing. Now, how about a three-point turn.'

Captain Blackpatch's three-point turn actually had four-and-a-half points in it, but Mrs Broadside didn't seem to mind, and only shut her eyes briefly. Nor did Mrs Broadside seem to mind when the Captain reversed into a pillar box and knocked it over. Mrs Broadside shut her eyes for several seconds and gave her head a little shake.

She didn't even seem worried when she asked the Captain what the speed limit on the High Street was, and he thought she wanted him to drive along it as fast as possible. They raced down the High Street at eighty-five miles an hour. This time, Mrs Broadside kept her eyes shut all the time and Captain Blackpatch was sure she was singing to herself – or maybe it was a little moan.

'Emergency stop!' cried Mrs Broadside, and Blackpatch threw the anchor out of the window. This time, it was not the bumper that came off, but the lamp-post that was wrenched from the ground and dragged behind with a lot of clanging and clattering.

They went back to the test centre where Mrs Broadside sat inside the truck, in silence, with her eyes still shut, for what seemed like ages. Captain Blackpatch pushed the battered

lamp-post to one side and bit his lip
nervously. Had he passed? At last Mrs
Broadside took a deep, deep breath, opened
her eyes and turned to the Captain.

'Mr Blackpatch, if I fail you on this test
you will probably come back and frighten
the living daylights out of me all over again.
I don't want that to happen, so I am going
to pass you, on one condition . . .'

'I am yours for ever, delightful woman!'
cried Blackpatch in an enthusiastic display
of relief.

'Go away! I don't want you to be mine for
one second, let alone for ever. I will pass
you only on the condition that if you ever

see me again you will drive away in the opposite direction. Is that understood?'

'If you insist.'

Mrs Broadside did insist. She got out of the truck and staggered into the test centre. Captain Blackpatch gave her a cheerful toot and drove back home. He screeched to a halt outside number 25 and leaped out of the truck.

'I won!' he yelled, jigging a little hornpipe up the path.

The other pirates came hurtling out of the house and crowded round their leader. 'Oh good,' shouted Bald Ben. 'Well done, Cap'n.'

Molly and Polly tugged at their gallant leader. 'Then we can have a treat after all.

What is it?' Captain Blackpatch grinned at their expectant faces.

'We are going on a holiday,' he announced.

'A holiday!' cried Lumpy Lawson. 'I've never had a holiday before.'

'Yes, a camping holiday,' added Blackpatch, 'with a proper tent and everything. It will be terrific.'

Blackpatch was only slightly wrong here. As things turned out, the holiday was not exactly 'terrific', but it was something beginning with 't-e-r-r', and it did have the same number of letters. But it was a word that meant something a lot different.

3 Trouble from Next Door

The campsite was large, and full of campers. There were big tents and little tents. There were trailer tents and tents on wheels. There were tents that looked like igloos and tents that looked like tepees . . . and then there was the Indoor Pirates' tent, and that looked like nothing on earth.

The pirates had never put up a tent before. Captain Blackpatch stood on the deck of the truck and shouted out instructions. 'That pole goes there, Lumpy. No, not in Ben's ear, you hopeless haddock! Down a bit . . . up a bit . . .'

But it was no use. Nobody really knew what they were

doing, not even the Captain. By the time they had finished, the tent was flat in one place and pointy in another. It was floppy in the middle and stretchy round the edges. It had a door in the roof and a plastic window

on the floor. Even Lumpy Lawson thought there were a few too many lumps in it. 'I don't think we've put it up properly,' he said.

'Why is the window on the bottom?' asked Polly. 'That's silly.'

'No it isn't,' Molly replied. 'That's so we can say "hello" to all the worms and things.'

'Nobody says "hello" to worms! You're stupid.'

'I'm not. You have to say "hello" to them, otherwise they'll think you're rude and they'll bite you.'

'Worms don't bite.'

'They'll bite *you*,' insisted Molly. 'They always bite horrible people, and they'll suck out all your bones and your body will go like jelly and you'll be all floppy and everyone will laugh at you and call you things like Polly-wobble and –'

'Pickled penguins!' roared Blackpatch.

'We are trying to put up a tent. We are not having a discussion about being polite to worms. I've had enough. I am going exploring to see where everything is, and by the time I come back I expect this tent to be put up properly.'

Blackpatch left the other pirates to get on with the hard work, while he went for a gentle stroll. His head was all in a bother and he needed a bit of peace and quiet so that it could un-bother itself.

It was an interesting campsite, full of twisty paths that wound their way among the many tents and caravans. Blackpatch hardly noticed, but as he strode along people popped out of their tents and pointed and whispered to each other. 'Pirates! There are pirates on the campsite!'

The Captain reached the far end of the camp, and there he made a very important discovery. The campsite was built next to a lake. It was a big blue lake, shimmering in the late-afternoon sun, but it was not the lake itself that caught the Captain's attention. It was what was in the middle of the lake.

There was an island – a small, wooded island. A hill crowned the middle, and a little beach ran all around its edge like a rim around a hat.

Now, although Captain Blackpatch didn't care for the sea, or lakes, or ponds, or puddles, or even little *drips* of water, he *did* like islands. As far as Captain Blackpatch knew there was only one reason for there being an island. Islands were there so that people could bury things on them. And the only things that people buried were valuable things – like treasure.

Looking across the shining water, Blackpatch could see people on the distant island. What were they doing? Surely they were digging? DIGGING! He screwed up his eyes and squinted hard, trying to focus them more clearly. The big question was: were the diggers putting something in, or taking something out?

A little boy ran past, stopped, came back slowly and then stood and stared at the Captain. 'Are you a *real* pirate?' he asked. Blackpatch glared down at him fiercely.

'I might be. Are those real binoculars hanging round your neck?' The boy nodded. 'In that case, I'm a real pirate and if you don't lend them to me I'll chop you up and make you into sausages.'

The boy, whose name was Jack, didn't budge, but merely asked what

kind of sausages. 'Pork and herb, or spicy beef?'

Captain Blackpatch grabbed the binoculars. 'Don't be so cheeky! You children are supposed to be scared of pirates. Haven't you seen Captain Hook in that film?'

'Yes, an' the crocodile got him and it'll get you too. Give me my binoculars back.' Jack made a grab for his binoculars.

'Don't snatch, you horribly small, squeaky person. Urgh! Half your front teeth are missing!'

'They came out and there are new ones growing. I bet you don't get new teeth when yours fall out, 'cos you're too old. Give me my binoculars or I'll tell my mum.'

'Will you stop snatching? I must see what they're doing on the island. I don't care if you tell the Queen Mother. I'm not scared of wimpy-pimpy women. Ah! Brilliant! They *are* burying something! We're going to be rich!' Blackpatch at last let go of the binoculars and Jack ran off.

The Captain hurried back to the tent and was surprised to find it looking just as it should. The door was in the right place, and so were the window, the ceiling, and the

floor. Lumpy Lawson had set up a barbecue. Bald Ben was gathering a little bunch of wild flowers but, best of all, there was no sign of the twins.

'They had an argument about who could run the furthest,' said Lumpy Lawson. 'They set off to find out and haven't come back yet. Oh, pimplepox! The flames have gone out again.'

'The lady next door put the tent up for us,' explained Bald Ben. 'She's ever so nice. I think she likes me.' Bald Ben's face cracked into a huge grin and he flushed red. 'She said I was just like a big baby.'

Blackpatch was about to point out to Ben that being called a big baby was not exactly a compliment, but he had far more important things to say. 'Come closer,' he whispered. 'Don't tell anyone, but I think there's treasure near by.'

'Treasure!' cried Bald Ben.

'Ssssh! I said don't tell *anyone*. There's a lake just over there with an island in the middle, and I saw someone burying something.'

Lumpy Lawson put some sausages on the barbecue. He frowned deeply. 'How are we going to get to the island?' he asked. 'Islands are surrounded by water. I don't like water.'

'None of us likes water,' Captain Blackpatch pointed out. 'But if we want the treasure we are going to have to get across to that island somehow. I want you both to keep an eye out for some way of getting to the island, OK?'

Bald Ben and Lumpy both nodded. Lumpy turned the sausages over and dropped three of them into the long grass. He tried picking them up but they were rather hot. 'Yakky-yoo! Ow! Ow!' He dropped the sausages back in the grass, speared them angrily with a fork and popped them back on the barbecue, covered with wisps of dry grass.

'They look nice,' observed the Captain tartly.

'Herbs,' muttered Lumpy, sucking his burnt fingers. 'They're sprinkled with herbs. Campers always eat their sausages like this.'

'I think I'll have mine without, thank you all the same,' growled the Captain.

There was a loud noise in the distance, and a moment later Polly and Molly appeared, still running. They flung themselves into the depths of the tent, and even before they could start quarrelling Blackpatch was looming over them with a menacing scowl. 'Don't say a word,' he hissed, 'or you won't get any supper, and it's sausages – special sausages with herbs.'

Luckily, the twins were too puffed out to argue with Blackpatch, themselves or anyone at all. Hardly had the twins settled down than the boy with the binoculars went strolling past, took one look at Blackpatch, and ran straight to his mother in the tent next door.

'Mum! Mum! That man tried to take my binoculars *an'* he said he'd make me into sausages an' he said he's not scared of wimpy-pimpy women.'

Jack's mother came striding out of her tent, her jaw set and fire flashing in her eyes. She went straight up to Blackpatch and stabbed him in the chest with a dagger-like finger. 'Who are you . . .' **poke!** '. . . calling a wimpy-pimpy woman?' **poke!** 'You listen to me . . .' **poke! poke!** 'If you hurt my son . . .' **poke!** '. . . I'll pull that silly hat down your head so far . . .' **poke!** '. . . that you'll be wearing it round your bony bottom like a skirt!' **poke!** 'Then we'll see who the wimpy-pimpy woman is!'

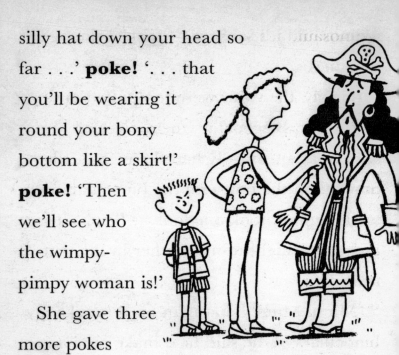

She gave three more pokes and Captain Blackpatch disappeared backwards into the back of the tent with a resounding crash. Jack's mother turned and stormed back to her own tent.

Bald Ben peered in at the Captain, who was lying in a crumpled heap on the floor.

'That was the lady who put up our tent,' he said. 'I told you she was nice.'

'She's not nice!' bellowed Blackpatch. 'And she's not a lady! She's a monster, a . . .

a dinosaur, a demon, a dragon!'

Bald Ben stood over the Captain with his big arm muscles twitching angrily. He shook his little bunch of flowers at Blackpatch. 'Don't you call her names,' he said. 'She put our tent up for us and that was very nice of her, and I like her and I picked these flowers for her!'

Captain Blackpatch groaned and sat up. 'Ben – you're a pirate! Pirates don't go round the place giving wimpy women bunches of flowers!'

'She can't have been that wimpy,' Bald Ben baldly pointed out. 'She sorted you out, didn't she?'

'I didn't want to hurt her,' snapped Blackpatch. 'Anyhow, we must keep an eye on her and that pesky Jack. He was with me when I saw the island and I think he spotted the treasure being buried too. I bet he's after it.'

Even Bald Ben realized that this might cause major trouble, and he stuck the flowers in a plastic mug, put them on the camping table and stared at them wistfully. Lumpy Lawson finished the barbecue and served up lumpy sausages to everyone, including the Captain. (Lumpy had dropped them again and now they had little clods of mud clinging to them, as well as grass.)

That night, the pirates lay rocking in their hammocks and whispering secret plans to each other. 'Tomorrow we must think of a way to reach the island,' muttered the Captain.

'We could build a raft,' suggested Polly.

'I've got a better idea,' Molly hissed, but Blackpatch smacked his lips crossly and pulled a long wisp of grass from between his teeth. 'Nice sausages, Lumpy,' he murmured, before turning over and falling into a deep, treasure-full sleep.

4 On the Treasure Trail

Lumpy Lawson reckoned his brain would burst from the top of his head if he thought any harder. Even the twins were looking vaguely pensive. It was breakfast time and the pirates were sitting round the camping table and trying to think of a good way to reach the island.

'What about a bridge?' suggested Bald Ben.

'Too difficult,' chorused the others.

'A submarine . . .' Lumpy offered, and was met with looks of speechless horror from the others. The mere thought of being right *under* the water was too much to bear.

'A raft,' said Polly. 'I said last night we should make a raft.'

'It was my idea first,' Molly claimed.

'It was *not*! It was my idea, and I said it,

and everybody heard me.'

'Yeah, but I *thought* of it before you; I just didn't say anything.'

'Well, it doesn't count if you don't *say*,' Polly shouted indignantly.

'Does!'

'Doesn't!'

With one accord, the other three pirates drew their swords and threatened the twins with instant death if they didn't shut up. Captain Blackpatch tugged thoughtfully at his pointy chin. 'We've got to get that treasure. We shall have to find some kind of boat.'

'But, Captain, you always get seasick,' Lumpy said gloomily.

'Surely you can't get seasick on a lake?' Ben wanted to know. 'I've never heard of anyone getting lake-sick. Anyhow, I've not seen any boats around here.'

Blackpatch impatiently drummed his fingers on the table. 'Neither have I. Maybe we shall be able to find one in the town.' This met with general approval so they clambered into, or on to, the truck and off they went to Bumpton, with the pirates bouncing about in the back very uncomfortably, all except for Captain Blackpatch who sat in the front and drove and felt very comfortable, thank you very much.

Bumpton was a holiday town. It was full of knick-knack shops and flags and balloons and noisy people. Blackpatch was looking for somewhere to park, but the only spot he

could find was marked 'DISABLED
DRIVERS ONLY'. Blackpatch screeched to
a halt. He jumped out of the truck, pulled
one arm from his jacket-sleeve and hid his
arm inside his jacket so that the sleeve
looked empty.

'That's cheating,' scolded Bald Ben.
Blackpatch rolled his eyes in despair.

'Ben, however did you
become a pirate? Pirates are
supposed to cheat . . . and rob,
and steal, and generally be
nasty.'

'Well, I don't think that's
very nice,' Ben muttered
moodily, and he trailed after
the others as they followed their
captain up the High Street.

Bumpton was not the best place to go for
a boat hunt. The pirates searched and
searched without success, until at last

Lumpy Lawson spotted something bright and boat-ish hanging in the window of a toyshop.

'Look, Captain! That's what we need.' And there it was – a bright yellow, inflatable dinghy. Blackpatch eyed it thoughtfully, and wondered how they could steal it.

'Lumpy, you go inside and keep the shop-keeper busy. When the right moment comes, we'll nip in and pinch the boat. Go on, do your stuff!'

Lumpy was pushed into the shop and the shop-keeper came forward to the counter with a smile. Lumpy's heart was in his mouth. What *was* he to do?

'Can I help you?' asked the shop-keeper.

'Oh, um, yes, oh – look!' Lumpy suddenly

pointed up behind the shop-keeper's head. 'There's a butterfly.' The shop-keeper turned and gazed up behind him for a moment. Lumpy beckoned frantically to the others who were still waiting outside, but Blackpatch just made faces back at him.

'Go on!' mouthed the Captain crossly.

'I can't see a butterfly,' said the shop-keeper, quite mystified. Lumpy tried again.

'Oh, look – there's a gorilla in a bikini!'

The shop-keeper turned and looked where Lumpy was pointing, but Blackpatch's sword had stuck in his belt and he was having an almighty struggle. Lumpy was beginning to panic.

'Oh, look!' he said for the third time. 'There's a piano on fire and I think you ought to put it out.'

The shop-keeper gazed steadily at Lumpy. 'I'm sorry, sir, but I don't understand what kind of game you're playing. Now, is there anything you want?' Lumpy gave up in despair.

'Yes,' he sighed. 'We'd like that yellow boat and my friend out there in the big hat will pay for it.' Blackpatch marched inside, cursing Lumpy.

'Oh, well done,' he hissed, and he handed over some money to the shop-keeper.

'It's not my fault,' whispered Lumpy. 'You should have come in the first time.'

The Captain was a bit confused when he was handed a small cardboard box by the shop-keeper.

'What's this?' he demanded suspiciously.

'It's your dinghy,' the shop-keeper replied.

'No it isn't. Mine is much, much bigger than this.'

'Yes, sir, but this one doesn't have any air in it yet. When you get it home you take it

50

out of the box and pump it up.'

Luckily, Ben had seen an inflatable dinghy before and managed to convince the Captain that the shop-keeper wasn't trying to trick him. 'Not everyone cheats,' said Bald Ben, rather self-righteously, as they left the shop.

On the way back to the truck, the pirates bought some spades so that they could dig up the treasure. (Blackpatch was not going to risk another useless robbery.) They could almost feel the treasure jingling in their pockets, and their spirits rose.

As soon as they got back to the campsite, the Indoor Pirates began to put their plan into action. Blackpatch set Molly and Polly blowing up the dinghy by mouth, which was very cunning of him because it meant they couldn't quarrel with each other. Lumpy Lawson lay in his hammock recovering from his dreadful ordeal in the toyshop, while

Bald Ben hung about next door's tent with a silly grin on his face.

'Hello,' he said, when he caught sight of Jack and his mum.

'Hello,' said Jack's mum. 'You look busy next door. What are you doing?'

'Us? Oh, we're going trea . . . I mean, no we're not,' he added hastily. 'We're not at all.'

'Not what?' asked Jack's mum.

'I bet you're going to that island to dig for treasure,' said Jack, turning to his mum. 'Can I go too?'

'I don't think so, Jack,' said his mum. 'You shouldn't be playing with pirates. They're not nice.'

Bald Ben was stung. He hated it when

people didn't think he was nice. 'I'm all right,' he insisted. 'Really. I kissed a baby once.'

Jack's mum laughed quietly. 'You're all right, Ben,' she admitted. 'It's that other one I don't like – Blackpatch.' Ben shuffled his feet.

'The Captain's not bad really. He likes to behave as if he's bad.'

'I noticed,' said Jack's mum coldly. A sudden thought occurred to Ben.

'Don't go away,' he cried and he raced back to the pirate-tent, grabbed the plastic mug with its little bunch of flowers and went panting back next door. He handed the mug to Jack's mum. 'These are for you,' he said.

'Ben! Thank you – you are sweet!' Jack's mum leaned forward on tiptoe and kissed him on the cheek. Ben grinned so hard his face almost split in half. Jack stared at them both, stuck two fingers in his mouth and said he was going to be sick.

Blackpatch began yelling for everyone. The dinghy was all blown up and everything was ready.

'Come on,' he cried, and strode off towards the lake, leaving the others to carry the spades and the oars and the dinghy. It was only when they reached the shore of the lake that they realized the dinghy was too small to carry all of them. 'Someone will have to stay behind,' said the Captain.

'I know,' cried Molly, 'we can do "eeny-meeny-miny-mo" and the last one out can't go and it will be Polly.'

'No!' Polly shouted. 'We won't do "eeny-meeny", we'll do "ip-dip-dip, my little ship", and Molly gets left behind.'

While the twins were busy shouting, the others loaded the spades into the dinghy and set off. They were already a little way from the shore when the sisters realized what had happened. 'That's not fair!' they both cried, and for once they were in agreement, but there was nothing they could do about it.

'You two can't swim,' Blackpatch pointed out, then suddenly turned green and put his head over the side. Bald Ben steadied the little boat.

'Oh dear, maybe you can get lake-sick after all. Be careful, Captain, don't lean too far over. Your weight is pulling down the side of the dinghy and water's getting in.'

The warning was too late. Water was already pouring into the dinghy, turning the bottom into a miniature paddling pool, and the more the pirates struggled, the more water came sloshing over the sides.

'Bumblepoo!' yelled Lumpy Lawson. 'I've got a soggy botty!'

Captain Blackpatch tried to stand. He waved frantically back at Molly and Polly. 'Save us!' he shouted. 'We're drowning!' The twins stared at each other. Emergency! But where was the nearest help?

'You go that way,' cried Polly. 'I'll go this way.'

'No! You go this way and I'll go that way!'

They set off, turned about, crashed into each other, set off again, turned round, crashed for a second time, got up, hit each other, crashed down, stood up, turned round, had another crash and ended up sprawling in the sand and trying to sit on each other's head.

Meanwhile, Blackpatch had fallen out of the dinghy with a loud SPLOSH! and found that the lake only came up to his knees. 'I'm not drowning!' he panicked, before realizing it was quite all right if he wasn't. He struggled to his feet. 'Hey, lads! It's all right – we're safe. We can paddle back to shore. Come on.'

Bald Ben and Lumpy struggled out of the dinghy, which now had a puncture and no longer looked like a boat at all, but more like a large and useless popped balloon. Ben tucked the spades under his arm and they waded back to the shore.

'Thank you for rescuing us,' Blackpatch told the twins icily, and he squelched up the beach and back to the tent. He went inside, did up the zip, changed his clothes and went to bed, while Ben and Lumpy stood outside shivering, without even a towel between them.

'Can we come in?' asked Ben.

'No. I'm ill. Go away,' snarled the Captain.

Jack appeared next to Ben and he tugged at the pirate's wet trousers. 'Mum says you can change in her tent and dry off and she promises she won't look.' So Ben and Lumpy went next door to change. Jack's mum only had some towels and frilly blouses for them to wear, but she did make them a nice cup of tea. She gave Jack and the twins a glass of cola each and she even made sure that the glasses were all *exactly* the same size.

'This is wonderful,' sighed Ben, giving Jack's mum a big smile. She winked at him and he almost fell off his camping chair.

'You've gone very red, Ben,' Lumpy said.

'Sunburn,' muttered Ben, and hid his face behind his mug of tea.

5 Blackpatch Has a Plan

'That dinghy was a fat lot of use,' grumbled Captain Blackpatch the next day.

'It was OK until you leaned over the side,' said Lumpy.

'Do you know what would have happened if I hadn't? I would have –'

'Maybe we can find another boat,' Bald Ben quickly suggested, and the Captain agreed.

'It's the only way we shall be able to get to that treasure. There must be a boat somewhere because I saw people on that island, and the only way they could have got there was if they had a boat.'

'They might have flown,' said Molly.

'Or floated down on a parachute,' said Polly.

'Or jumped,' Molly put in. Polly wrinkled her nose.

'Jumped? Don't be stupid. Nobody could jump that far.'

'Well then,' Molly sneered, 'if Nobody can jump that far perhaps it was Nobody who was on the island.'

'I'VE GOT AN IDEA!' roared Blackpatch, with his face fixed in his fiercest frown ever. 'Why don't we tie the twins up and leave them here while we go boat hunting in peace?'

'That's a good idea,' said Ben.

'That *is* a good idea!' agreed Lumpy, and they grabbed the girls, tied them back to back, and left them sitting by the tent looking thunderous from head to toe. Blackpatch gave them a parting smile.

'You see what can be done when people agree with each other instead of quarrelling! See you later, twins.'

The Indoor Pirates wandered down to the lake and once again found themselves staring wistfully across to the little island. The wood on the hill looked dark and green and secretive.

'I bet there's heaps of treasure buried over there,' Blackpatch said dreamily.

'Heaps . . .' murmured Lumpy, who was almost in a trance.

Bald Ben tugged at the Captain's sleeve. 'What's that thing on the water over there?' He pointed just round the corner of the lake near the campsite. 'It's not a swan, is it?'

'No, it isn't,' agreed the Captain, 'unless it's a swan with two heads. I think we had better investigate. Keep quiet, and crouch down in case someone sees.'

The three pirates crept round the edge of

the lake. The closer they got to the strange
thing the more astonished they became. A
peculiar noise drifted across the water . . .
schukka-schikka-squeak-schikka, schukka-
schikka-squeak-schikka.

'Shivering shrimps! It's a . . . boaty-
thingy-whatsit!' cried Blackpatch, and it was
too. On board the boaty-thingy-whatsit
were Jack and his mum. They were sitting
down and pedalling hard. What a strange
machine!

Jack's mum saw the pirates crouching by

the shore and called out to them from the pedalo she was riding. 'Hello, Ben!'

Ben was about to wave back cheerfully when Blackpatch seized him by the shoulder and pulled him down into the long grass. 'Get down!' he hissed. 'Before she spots you.'

'She already has spotted me. She only said "hello", and I was only going to say "hello" back.'

'Don't be stupid. She could be spying on us.'

Jack stood on his seat. 'Why are you all hiding in the grass?' he asked. 'Have you got a secret or something?' This was too much for Blackpatch, and he leaped up.

'We're not hiding,' he declared.

'You were,' said Jack. 'You were crouching in the grass.'

'No we weren't,' shouted Blackpatch. 'We fell over, that's what.' Jack's mum laughed.

'All of you – at the same time?'

'They didn't fall, Mum,' Jack insisted. 'They were hiding.'

'Why is that child so clever?' Blackpatch hissed under his breath. 'Nobody should be as clever as that. It's not natural.' He called out to the pair and asked them what their boaty-thing was.

'It's a pedalo,' said Jack, and he explained how it worked.

Blackpatch studied the small craft carefully. It was rather small and wobbly and it looked as if you could fall out all too easily. The Captain's stomach went queasy at the thought of taking to the water again so soon after his last little escapade.

However, there didn't seem to be any other choice, and gradually a cunning smile slid across beneath his pointy nose.

Blackpatch pulled the other two further along the beach until they could see the tiny pedalo harbour. There they counted ten pedalos altogether. Some were out on the lake and others were roped to a little jetty. Two men were standing on the jetty, taking people's money and showing them to their pedalos.

Captain Blackpatch's eyes narrowed to sneaky slits. 'We are going to be rich, lads,' he whispered. 'We are going to be very rich and it is all going to happen tonight.'

'Tonight?' repeated Lumpy. 'Have you got a plan, Captain?' Blackpatch nodded.

'We come down here tonight, on tiptoe,

very, very quietly, when everyone is asleep . . .'

'Will we be asleep?' asked Ben, who liked a good night's snooze.

'Of course not! We shall be out here, doing a bit of skulduggery.'

'What's skulduggery?' Ben asked, hoping that it didn't mean having to be nasty to anyone.

'Skulduggery is what pirates do at night,' explained Blackpatch. 'Stop asking awkward questions. Listen, we come down here tonight and we steal some pedalos. Then we nip across to the island and dig up the treasure and come back here and . . .' Blackpatch broke off and beamed knowingly at the others.

'Go to sleep?' Ben finished hopefully.

'No! We'll have the treasure, won't we? We shall be rich! We run away with the treasure and live happily ever after.'

'And *then* we go to sleep,' Ben added with a smile.

'Yes, Ben, after that you can sleep for a thousand years if you want, in a bed as big as a bandstand and as soft as duck-down.'

'Wow!' breathed Ben rapturously.

'Come on,' urged the Captain. 'We must get back to the twins and tell them what the plan is.'

Back on the campsite, there was a bit of a commotion going on. Jack and his mum had finished their pedalo ride and gone back to their tent, only to discover that Polly and Molly were rolling about tied back to back. They were covered in dirt and grass and furiously kicking their legs in the air.

'Those poor pirate children,' said Jack's mum. 'How on earth did they get in that state?'

'The Captain tied us up!' cried Polly.

68

'Yeah, an' Lumpy and Ben!' shouted Molly.

'That's dreadful,' said Jack's mum, hastily untying them. 'You poor things. Jack, get Molly and Polly a drink. Those pirates aren't fit to look after themselves, let alone two children.'

Molly and Polly slurped down their drinks in no time at all and then played with Jack. He proudly showed them his paddling toy. It was an enormous green inflatable crocodile, with handles down the back that

you could hold on to while you sat on it and
paddled. 'My gran gave it to me,' Jack said.

'It's enormous,' said Polly.

'It's huge,' said Molly.

'That's just what I said,' Polly pointed
out.

'No – you said "enormous" and I said
"huge".'

'Yeah? They mean the same thing –'

'No they don't. Huge is bigger than
enormous.'

'It is *not*! Enormous is much bigger than
huge. Enormous is as big as, as big as . . .
the whole universe!' cried Polly. Molly
folded her arms in triumph.

'In that case, this crocodile can't be
enormous, or it would be as big as the
universe and it wouldn't even fit in this
tent,' she declared. 'And that means it's
huge – like I said.'

'Girls!' laughed Jack's mum. 'It doesn't

matter how big it is. If you ask Jack nicely I'm sure he'll let you have a go on it tomorrow.' Her soft face suddenly became tense. 'The other pirates are coming back. Good – I want a word with them.'

What took place after that wasn't very nice – at least it certainly was not very nice for Ben and Lumpy and Blackpatch. Jack's mum was furious at the way they had left the twins all tied up, and she made it quite clear that she thought they were monsters. Blackpatch carefully stood behind Ben and Lumpy so that if this dreadful woman started poking with her finger again they would get the worst of it.

But Bald Ben didn't care how much he got poked. He was overcome

with despair when he discovered that the
nice lady from next door was so cross with
him. He gazed at her with huge puppy-dog
eyes. He felt as if his whole world had
collapsed and he didn't care how rich he
was going to be.

Molly and Polly came out of Jack's tent
and sauntered cockily past the stunned
pirates. 'She told you!' hissed Molly with
immense satisfaction.

'Yeah,' agreed Polly, and the two sisters
turned to each other and slapped their
hands together like a pair of jubilant
footballers. The other

pirates gawked
at each other.
Did they really see
what they had just
seen? Incredible!

6 Treasure Island at Last

In the dead of night, the Indoor Pirates crept out of their tent. 'Are you ready?' hissed Captain Blackpatch. 'Are you all on tiptoe?'

'Yes, Cap'n.'

'Good – follow me.' He turned to go and almost leaped out of his skin as he came face to face with a huge green monster.

'Aaargh!' Blackpatch was trembling in his boots. He clung to Bald Ben like a scared monkey and pointed at the green beast with its snapping jaws and great white fangs.

'It's only Jack's inflatable crocodile,' said Lumpy. 'He goes paddling on it.'

Blackpatch glared at the toy perched against Jack's tent. 'That child will be the death of me,' he muttered, then set off once more, creeping past the other tents. This time they reached the lake without further incident and quietly crept on to the jetty. The pedalos were still and silent, floating on the dark waters of the lake. Blackpatch climbed on a pedalo, sat down and hunted for the rope that tied it to the jetty, only to discover to his horror that it wasn't tied with a rope any longer.

A heavy chain fastened the pedalo to a stake, and the heavy chain had an even heavier padlock clamped through the links.

'They're all locked up!' he cried. 'Stupid, stupid people! Why have they chained them up?'

'I suppose they don't want anyone to steal them,' said Bald Ben, who thought it was a very sensible thing to do. Blackpatch swiped his hat from his head and began battering Ben with it.

'You cod-brained bladder-wrack! Of course they don't want anyone to steal them, but we've got to get to Treasure Island, and now we can't.'

Polly and Molly had got an idea, and it was quite a good one. 'Why don't we use Jack's crocodile?' said Molly, and her sister nodded. 'It's probably big enough for all of us, and we can use the spades as paddles.'

Blackpatch allowed this neat idea to roll about his brain for a few moments. What a wonderful way to get even with that smart little clever-clogs from the tent next door – they could use his favourite toy to grab the treasure! 'Right, lads – back to the campsite – everyone on tiptoe again.'

Off they went, creeping back to Jack's tent where the green beast was still standing on its tail and looking menacing by moonlight. Lumpy took the front end of the crocodile and Blackpatch took the tail because, even though it was made of plastic, the Captain didn't like to get right next to those sharp teeth. A little voice came from the tent. 'Who's that out there?' Jack asked sleepily.

'Nobody,' hissed Blackpatch. 'Go back to sleep or I'll chop your ears off.' This met with silence so the pirates set off for the lake. On the way there they had a stroke of luck because Bald Ben spotted an inflatable duck outside another tent.

'That will do me nicely,' he told the others. 'I don't like crocodiles – too many teeth.'

Back at the campsite, Jack lay in his bed dreamily thinking to himself. There must have been somebody outside 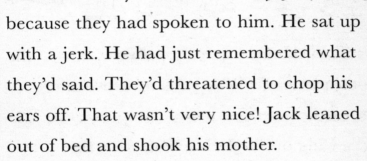 because they had spoken to him. He sat up with a jerk. He had just remembered what they'd said. They'd threatened to chop his ears off. That wasn't very nice! Jack leaned out of bed and shook his mother.

'Mum? Mum? Someone is outside and they said that if I didn't go to sleep they'd cut off my ears.'

This was quite enough to put Jack's mum on red-alert and she rose from her bed like an Amazon warrior and threw herself outside with an angry yell. 'Who wants to chop off my son's ears?' she demanded, and was surprised to find nobody there.

This changed quickly, because the
occupants of all the tents near by were
roused by her shout and campers came
crawling out in their pyjamas and
nightgowns demanding to know what was
going on, and waving torches in all
directions.

'Somebody has been prowling around,'
said Jack's mum accusingly. Jack came
outside, took one look and burst into tears.

'My crocodile's been stolen!' he wailed.

Jack's mum strode across to the pirates'

tent and poked her head inside. 'Just as I thought. There's nobody here. The pirates must have stolen Jack's crocodile.'

'My spotty duck's gone too,' cried an elderly lady. 'Come on, they must have taken them to the lake. Let's get after them!' With a cry of 'Get the pesky pirates!' the campers hurried off to the lake.

The Indoor Pirates were doing quite well. Blackpatch, Lumpy and Polly were sitting on the giant crocodile, merrily paddling away. The Captain was so excited at the thought of all the treasure that he quite

forgot to worry about being seasick, or lake-sick, or any kind of sick. Molly and Ben were on the duck, and they all found that the spades made excellent paddles. It did not take them long to reach the island. The pirates leaped ashore and scrambled up the beach.

'Treasure Island!' cried Blackpatch. 'At last!'

'Treasure Island!' echoed the others. 'Where do we dig, Cap'n?'

Captain Blackpatch studied the beach carefully. 'I reckon it must have been about here.' He prodded the sand with his spade. 'Get digging!'

The pirates set to with gusto, each digging in a different place. Sand was flying in every direction and soon Molly and Polly were back to their usual antics. 'Every time you take sand out of your hole you throw it into mine,' Polly complained.

'I'm only giving you your sand back,' said Molly, 'because you took it from your hole and put it in mine first of all.'

'Just dig,' bellowed Blackpatch. 'We're here to find treasure, not to argue.'

The pirates dug and dug. They dug here and they dug there, without finding so much as a pebble. They were almost ready to give up when Lumpy's spade struck something hard. 'I've found it, Captain!' he cried. 'There's a lump down here!'

The Indoor Pirates gathered round Lumpy's pit and watched with round eyes as he pushed his spade deep into the sand and began to lever out something large. The sand heaved and broke and trickled off the spade leaving the treasure in full view of everyone.

'It's . . .' began Blackpatch. 'It's . . .' He couldn't believe his eyes.

'It's rubbish,' muttered Bald Ben. 'Someone has been here and they've had a barbecue and a picnic and they've buried all their rubbish.'

The five pirates stared into the hole at their broken dreams. At the bottom of the pit lay a pile of burnt charcoal, several scraggy meat bones, some very sandy sandwiches (half-eaten) and some rotting bits of tomato and lettuce.

'I thought you said they'd buried treasure,' Lumpy accused the Captain.

'How was I to know they were burying rubbish?' cried Blackpatch angrily. 'I mean, what a stupid, stupid, STUPID thing to bury! Why would anyone bury rubbish?!'

'So it doesn't make a mess, of course,' Bald Ben said.

A shout drifted across the water from the distant shore. 'There they are, on the island! After them!' The campers poured on to the jetty. Someone produced a key and the pedalos were unchained. Brandishing their torches like clubs, the campers began pedalling across the lake at full speed, with Jack and his mum in the lead and foam spurting from the churning paddles.

Captain Blackpatch turned white. 'Don't let that horrible pokey woman anywhere near me!' he cried, and he leaped on to Jack's crocodile. Lumpy and Polly joined him and they desperately tried to escape the fast-approaching armada of pedalos. Ben and Molly were close behind on their giant spotted duck, paddling furiously.

'Faster, faster!' cried Blackpatch, his spade flashing in the water, and he gripped the crocodile with his legs to stop himself slipping off.

Unfortunately, he squeezed the inflatable toy so hard that the crocodile could no longer contain itself. The bung suddenly shot from its tail and a jet of air screeched out, sending the crocodile skimming across the water with the pirates hanging on for dear life. 'Help!' yelled Blackpatch, as the jet-propelled croc went whizzing backwards and forwards and round and round like a crazy balloon. Up and down it went, with the air rushing from its tail – SPLURRRRRRRRRR!!!

At last it ran out of wind, went completely floppy and left the pirates floundering in the water. Blackpatch discovered that this time the lake didn't come up to his knees but well above his hat.

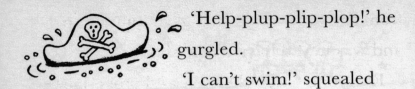 'Help-plup-plip-plop!' he gurgled.

'I can't swim!' squealed Polly, and she couldn't.

'I'll save you!' Molly shouted.

'But you can't swim either!' spluttered Polly, vanishing beneath the surface.

'Yes I can!' cried Molly and bravely dived in, sank and reappeared briefly. 'No I can't!' she agreed and sank again.

There was a loud splash as Jack's mum threw herself from her pedalo and dived into the black water. A moment later she reappeared with both twins, who immediately spurted fountains of water from their mouths, along with one or two startled fish. As the pedalos reached the pirates, other hands grabbed Blackpatch and Lumpy and pulled them from the water. Bald Ben gave himself up and was towed back to the shore.

Everyone was rather wet and cross. Jack's mum confronted a very bedraggled Captain Blackpatch. 'You'd cut off my son's ears, would you?' **Poke!** 'We'll see about that!' **Poke!** She reached up, grabbed the Captain's ears and gave them a good pull.

'Yow!' he cried.

Jack smiled and looked up at the pirate

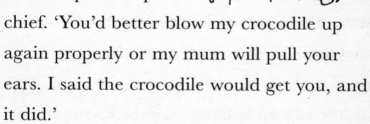

chief. 'You'd better blow my crocodile up again properly or my mum will pull your ears. I said the crocodile would get you, and it did.'

'It's your mum that's the crocodile,' hissed Blackpatch and everyone burst out laughing.

The campers went back to bed, and so did the pirates, all except for Blackpatch. He was left on his own, huffing and puffing

all night long. By the time morning came,
the crocodile was fully inflated and
Blackpatch was lying next to it, fully
deflated and snoring his hat off.

Bald Ben went to next door's tent. 'I'm
sorry about last night,' he mumbled
sheepishly, and he explained about the
treasure hunt.

'You are a big baby,' said Jack's mum.
'Fancy wanting to play with a plastic
crocodile. However did you get to be a
pirate?'

'My mum was a pirate and my dad was a
pirate. They taught me everything I know.'

'It wasn't much, was it?' laughed Jack's mum. Jack grabbed Ben by the hand.

'When I grow up I'm going to be a pirate,' he said, and his mother sighed.

'See what you've started?' But she gave Ben a bright smile and he came over all funny and turned red from head to toe. He went back to the pirate tent feeling a great deal happier.

Captain Blackpatch had woken up and was  now slumped back against Jack's crocodile. 'This holiday has been terrible,' he complained. 'There's been no treasure at all. Maybe it's time we went home.' But the other pirates didn't feel like going home. They were just getting used to camping. Lumpy had even stopped dropping the sausages in the grass.

'Can't we stay a bit longer?' they pleaded. Blackpatch gazed moodily back at them.

At that moment, Jack came across from his tent. He had his binoculars round his neck. He had a wooden sword stuck in his belt and a red spotted scarf tied on his head. 'I'm a pirate,' he declared, 'and I'm going on a treasure hunt. Who's coming with me?'

'Me!' cried Lumpy and Ben and the twins, and they set off at once. Blackpatch watched them for a few seconds.

'Wait for me!' he yelled and hurried after them.